The Guest Who Threw Tomatoes

By Cal Fussman

With Illustrations by
Lucy Schaeffer

The Sapikowskis didn't quite know what to expect when they went to the airport to pick up their guest. They had never met anyone from Spain.

"Remember," Mrs. Sapikowski said to Lauren and Adam, "we want our guest to feel at home. In Spain, they have different customs. This is a great opportunity to learn about Pepe's culture. And I'm sure it will be fun showing him ours."

Lauren and Adam were very excited about Pepe's arrival. What did people from Spain look like? Lauren wondered. What did they eat? What games did they like to play?

Adam knew it was special to have a Spanish guest because his parents allowed him to stay up until 10 o'clock to pick up Pepe at the airport.

As they waited, Mr. Sapikowski pulled out a little Spanish dictionary and practiced saying the word "*hola.*" That means "hello" in Spanish.

Mr. Sapikowski knew that Pepe had learned to speak English in school. But he thought Pepe might feel more at home if he greeted him in Spanish.

Just then, a loudspeaker announced that the flight from Spain had landed. Soon, a man wearing a funny black hat and a red cape appeared.

"I am Pepe from Spain," he said, with a great bow.

Nobody had ever bowed to Mrs. Sapikowski before. She was very impressed to have such a polite guest. Lauren and Adam bowed back.

"*Hola,*" Mr. Sapikowski said.

"*Hola,*" Pepe replied. "You are longer than a day without bread."

Now, Mr. Sapikowski was a very tall man. But he had never heard anyone say that about him before.

"It is an old Spanish expression," Pepe explained.

Mr. Sapikowski smiled at the compliment.

They picked up Pepe's luggage and began to drive home.

"Are you hungry?" Mrs. Sapikowski asked Pepe.

"Why, of course!" Pepe said. "It is 10 o'clock. That is the normal time to eat dinner, is it not?"

"Dinner at 10 o'clock at night!" Adam exclaimed. "I'd be sleeping when I ate supper if I lived in Spain."

"We usually eat dinner at 6:30," said Mr. Sapikowski. "But because this is such a special occasion, we'll all have another dinner."

"YAAAAAAAAAAAAAAAY!" Lauren and Adam cheered.

"Please allow me to cook my famous *tortillas*," Pepe said. "I insist!"

"Well," said Mrs. Sapikowski, "if you insist."

When they got home, Pepe began to crack eggs. He chopped up potatoes and peppers. Then he started to fry the *tortillas*. Soon, a wonderful aroma filled the house.

"This is delicious," Mr. Sapikowski said after his first bite.

"Feel free to cook anytime you'd like," Mrs. Sapikowski said.

Adam couldn't believe it. It was almost midnight and his parents were letting him stay up. "This is like a party!" he exclaimed.

"We in Spain are very famous for our parties," Pepe said. "They are called *fiestas*. Let me tell you all about them."

Mrs. Sapikowski cleared her throat. "That would be wonderful, Pepe," she said. "But the children have school tomorrow. It's time for them to go to bed."

"Oh, noooooooooo," groaned Lauren and Adam.

"Don't worry," Mrs. Sapikowski said. "Pepe will be here for three whole days. He'll tell you all about the Spanish *fiestas* after school tomorrow."

The next morning, while the children were at school, Mrs. Sapikowski took Pepe to the supermarket. He bought rice and chicken and fish. But mostly he bought tomatoes. He bought so many tomatoes, they nearly spilled out of the back of the Sapikowskis' minivan.

Mrs. Sapikowski thought this was a bit odd. But she kept silent, remembering how good Pepe's *tortillas* tasted.

That afternoon, Adam and Lauren ran home from school. They couldn't wait to hear about the *fiestas*.

Pepe took off his cape and hat. "These are what a bullfighter wears," he said. "But I must change to teach you about *La Fiesta de San Fermin*. Do you have some pencils?"

Adam and Lauren ran for the pencils.

Pepe carefully placed one behind each of his ears so that they were like the horns of a bull. Then he tied a green band around his head to keep the horns in place.

"*La Fiesta de San Fermin* is what people call The Running of the Bulls," Pepe said. "People line up behind a fence in a town called Pamplona. On the other side of the fence are many bulls. The bulls do not like to be trapped. It makes them very angry. When the fence is opened, the bulls come running out and the people must run through the streets to escape. The idea is not to get stuck by the horns of the bulls coming behind you."

Lauren and Adam looked at each other, their eyes wide with fright.

"It's a lot of fun," said Pepe. "Now, let's play."

Pepe got down on his hands and knees behind the sofa and began to snort. Lauren and Adam could see the pencils sticking up over the cushions like a bull's horns. All of a sudden, Pepe came charging.

"YIIIIIIIIIKES!" Adam screamed. "Run for your life!"

Lauren did just that.

Adam ran out of the playroom with Pepe in hot pursuit. The pencil-horns were an inch away as he raced into the kitchen. Adam jumped on top of the table to escape. He skidded right into the fruit bowl, which tumbled off the table and sent pears, apples and bananas scattering just ahead of Pepe the bull, who stepped on a banana and sent the fruit flying out of the peel. The banana smashed into the TV screen like a missile. Meanwhile, Lauren skidded on the peel and flipped onto the couch.

"YIIIIIIIIIIIIIIKES!" Adam cried, pushing dining room chairs over in front of Pepe the bull.

Lauren squealed with delight. What a fun game this was! She jumped off the couch and scooted into the laundry room.

Pepe was about to get her when his head smashed into the hamper.

Adam and Lauren ran for the bedroom. Pepe snorted after them. Mattresses flipped, pillow feathers flew, the toy chest tumbled and stuffed animals scattered. Finally, Adam, Lauren and the bull collapsed in the living room.

"*La Fiesta de San Fermin* is so much fun!" Lauren said, trying to catch her breath.

"Yeah," Adam said, rubbing his behind.

"I am so happy you enjoyed it," Pepe said. "Tomorrow, I will teach you about *La Tomatina*. But now, it is time for my *siesta*."

"Is a *siesta* like a *fiesta*?" Lauren asked.

"No, a *siesta* is a nap in the afternoon," Pepe explained. "Everyone takes a nap in the afternoon in Spain. Don't you?"

Pepe just couldn't believe that Lauren and Adam didn't take a *siesta* every day. He waved goodbye and went to his room for a nap.

Just then, Mrs. Sapikowski came in. She had been outside tending to her prized petunias. "What happened?" she cried, seeing all the laundry scattered about, the pillow feathers floating in the air and the chairs upside down as if a hurricane had blown through the house.

Lauren and Adam looked at each other. Lauren waited for Adam to explain. Adam waited for Lauren to explain. But neither one of them could say it first, so nobody said anything at all.

"We can't have the house looking like this in front of our guest," Mrs. Sapikowski said. "He's so polite—quick, clean up this instant!"

The next morning, Pepe asked Mrs. Sapikowski to take him to town to buy some goggles. Mrs. Sapikowski thought that was a fine idea. She had overheard Adam and Lauren telling Pepe about the big pool at the YMCA. Perhaps they would all go swimming.

Mrs. Sapikowski took Pepe into town. "I must stop at the cleaners," she said as she left Pepe at the sporting goods shop. "I'll be right back."

When she returned, Pepe was holding a huge sack. Mrs. Sapikowski wondered why he needed such a big bag for a tiny pair of goggles. But she didn't want her guest to think American women were nosey, so she didn't ask.

That afternoon, Lauren and Adam ran home from school to find out about *La Tomatina*.

Pepe was waiting outside with the huge sack next to many boxes of tomatoes. He did not have his red cape on, or even his funny hat. He was wearing the old clothes Mr. Sapikowski used to paint the house.

"In order for me to teach you about *La Tomatina*," Pepe said, "we will need the help of your friends. Get as many as you can."

So Lauren and Adam went around the neighborhood and brought back Dylan and Douglas and Michelle and Kenya and Katy and Emily and Olivia and Paul and Sarah and Yun and Elliott and Carol-Anne and Kiara.

All the kids gathered around Pepe.

"*La Tomatina* is a *fiesta* that takes place in a town called Buñol every August," Pepe told them.

"BOOON-YOL!" they repeated.

"Nobody is really sure how it started," Pepe continued. "It's said that two friends got into an argument at a fruit stand. One picked up a tomato and threw it at the other. The other started to throw tomatoes back and . . .

"Now, 50,000 people come to Buñol every August. They bring goggles to protect their eyes. Giant trucks drop tomatoes on the streets and the people

throw them at each other for a whole hour."

"Cooooooooooool!" said Douglas.

Pepe turned over the bag and let a bunch of goggles spill out. The kids strapped them on. Then Pepe picked up a tomato and squished it over Adam's head. Red pulp oozed down Adam's brow to the tip of his nose.

"EWWWWWWWW!" the boys and girls screamed. Adam got really mad. He picked up a tomato and threw it at Pepe. But Pepe ducked and the tomato hit Douglas in the chest. Douglas grabbed a tomato and threw it at Adam, but he missed and it hit Michelle. That made her really mad and so she grabbed three tomatoes and threw them, but it's hard to aim three tomatoes and so none hit Adam. They hit Kiara and Katy and Olivia instead. Olivia ran toward the box of tomatoes but slipped on the seeds and everyone laughed. She clenched her teeth, got up and fired a tomato at Lauren's behind. Bull's-eye! Before you knew it, everybody was throwing tomatoes at everybody else. Elliott even squished a tomato and dropped it down Paul's pants.

Mrs. Sapikowski was tending to her prized petunias when she heard the commotion. She lifted her head to see what was going on.

A tomato whizzed by her ear. She quickly ducked under her petunias.

Douglas' dad heard the noise. He came striding across the street and got hit right in the forehead. But he didn't get mad. He smiled and started throwing tomatoes too!

Soon, all the neighbors were running over and throwing tomatoes until there were no more left and everybody was swimming in tomato soup.

Just then, Mr. Sapikowski came home from work.

"What in tarnation is going on here?" he asked, looking at the river of red juice dripping down the side of his house.

Mrs. Sapikowski lifted her head. "Is the coast clear?" she asked.

"Oh, we just had a great tomato fight," said Douglas' dad.

"It's called *La Tomatina*," Adam explained.

"We also have a grape-throwing festival in Spain," said Pepe. "But I believe it's much more fun with tomatoes."

Douglas smiled and said, "It's soooooooooo coooooooooool!"

"Tomorrow," Pepe announced to everyone, "I invite you all here to learn about *La Fiesta de Santo Antonio*!"

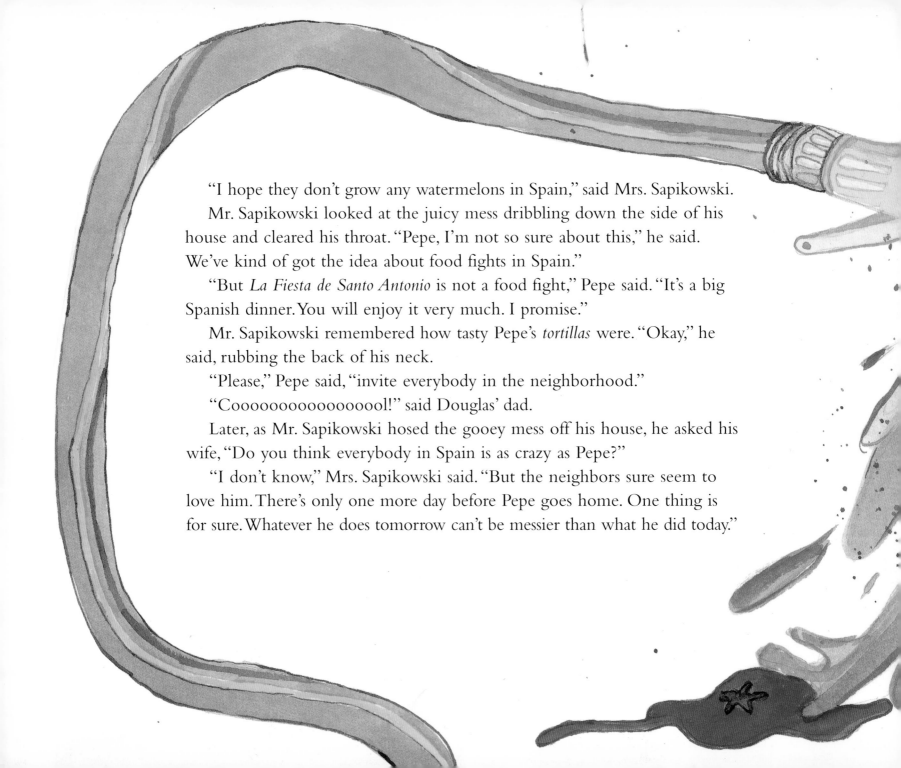

"I hope they don't grow any watermelons in Spain," said Mrs. Sapikowski.

Mr. Sapikowski looked at the juicy mess dribbling down the side of his house and cleared his throat. "Pepe, I'm not so sure about this," he said. We've kind of got the idea about food fights in Spain."

"But *La Fiesta de Santo Antonio* is not a food fight," Pepe said. "It's a big Spanish dinner. You will enjoy it very much. I promise."

Mr. Sapikowski remembered how tasty Pepe's *tortillas* were. "Okay," he said, rubbing the back of his neck.

"Please," Pepe said, "invite everybody in the neighborhood."

"Coooooooooooooooool!" said Douglas' dad.

Later, as Mr. Sapikowski hosed the gooey mess off his house, he asked his wife, "Do you think everybody in Spain is as crazy as Pepe?"

"I don't know," Mrs. Sapikowski said. "But the neighbors sure seem to love him. There's only one more day before Pepe goes home. One thing is for sure. Whatever he does tomorrow can't be messier than what he did today."

The next morning, Pepe borrowed the Sapikowskis' car to get the things needed for the party. He brought back a big pot and filled it with rice and chicken and sausage and fish. Then he built a fire and began to cook. The aroma wafted over the neighborhood.

Lauren and Adam and their friends carried tables and chairs over from the neighbors' houses. Soon, there was hardly room to move inside the Sapikowskis' house. But Mrs. Sapikowski couldn't complain, because the neighbors were so excited. At 4 o'clock, they filled every seat.

"This is a famous Spanish dish," Pepe said. "It's called *paella*."

Everybody shouted PI-YAAY-YAAAH! Then they began to eat.

"UMMMMMM! This is delicious!" the neighbors nodded to each other.

"We serve it in a village called Pavias every January on *La Fiesta de Santo Antonio*," Pepe said. "The mayor of Pavias invites everybody in town to his home for the dinner."

The neighbors all smiled at Mr. Sapikowski. That made Mr. Sapikowski very proud. He felt like he was the mayor of Estes Hills.

Just then there was a scream! It came from Michelle at a table next to the laundry room. Something furry and wet had brushed her leg under the table. Now all the boys and girls were screaming. Something wet and gooey and furry was going crazy under the table.

Mr. Sapikowski couldn't believe his eyes. Mrs. Sapikowski almost fainted.

It was a real live pig running around under the table!

Everyone jumped on top of the tables. Rice and chicken got knocked over. Soda spilled. Sausages scattered. The frightened pig ran into the laundry room and then ran out in a panic with Adam's freshly cleaned underwear on its head.

Oh, how the boys and girls laughed at the pig in Adam's underwear! Douglas tried to get the pig in a bear hug, but it slipped right through his arms. The pig had been smeared all over with grease!

Dylan dove for the pig, but it spurted away, flew through the air with the underwear on its head and knocked Douglas' mom into the big pot of PI-YAAY-YAAAH.

Finally, after every table and chair had been knocked over and the carpet was covered with chunks of chicken and fish and everybody had stopped laughing because it had started to hurt their bellies, Pepe put on gloves and picked up the pig.

"The running of the pig is the best part of *La Fiesta de Santo Antonio*," Pepe said, removing the underwear and patting the pig on its head.

"Cooooooooooool!" said Douglas and his mom and dad all together.

The next day, everyone in the neighborhood went to the airport to wish Pepe a good trip back to Spain.

"I am sorry I did not have time to teach you a dance called *flamenco*," Pepe told them. "But you are welcome to come to my home and learn."

"*Adios*," Lauren and Adam said. They had learned to say goodbye in Spanish.

"*Gracias*," Pepe said, meaning "thanks." Then he twirled in his cape and boarded the plane.

The Sapikowskis drove home. Mrs. Sapikowski was looking forward to a few days of peace and rest. But it felt too quiet. "Do you think everyone in Spain is as crazy as Pepe?" she asked.

"I don't know," Mr. Sapikowski said. "I guess we'd have to go to Spain to find out."

"Can we, Mom?" Lauren asked.

"Pepe invited us!" Adam said. "Can we go? PLEEEASE?"

The Sapikowskis decided to visit Pepe during summer vacation. They did not know if everyone in Spain was as crazy as Pepe. But as they boarded the plane, they were all wearing red capes and funny black hats. Just in case.

Thank You

This book is dedicated to our parents:
Rita & Herbert Fussman   Paula & Bill Schaeffer
We would also like to thank:

Gloria Wendy Sarah Adam Agnethe Michael Tio Arturo Suzy Soraya Lauren Nippa Gabriela Don Claire Maggie Savi Conrad Orville Gary Cem Sally Dave Nanny Nicky Larry Mr. Brown Jennifer Jim Linda Lisa Oliver Graaaanjay Stephanie Dylan Keilah Bridgette Bordeaux Mrs. Chianese's & Mrs. Willingmyre's first-grade class Andy Darby Iciar Sallie Robertito Steve Allison Noah Jessica Asa Jenny Elisha Professor Reed The Cheenies Gang Coaches Wooden & Bowden Erin Mary & Emma Kirsten Edisa Eisner, Branson & Steinbrenner Herbie Donna & Jimmy Lilian and, of course, Guy de Maupassant

This is a  book.

ISBN 0-9712695-0-5